*"The tiger leaps and the swallow
dips her wings in dark pools on the
other side of the world."*

To David and Gretta,
A.E.

International Standard Book No.
0–8120–6270–1 (hardcover)
0–8120–4828–8 (paperback)
Library of Congress Catalog Card No.
91–33201

**Library of Congress
Cataloging-in-Publication Data**

Edmiston, Jim.
  Mizzy and the tigers/Jim Edmiston and
Andy Ellis. — 1st ed. for the U.S. and
Canada.
      p. cm.
  Summary: When Mizzy, a cat lover and
wizard's daughter, learns that the jungle
houses cats bigger than her beloved Zigzag,
she ventures into the jungle to find a tiger.
  ISBN 0–8120–6270–1 (hardcover). —
ISBN 0–8120–4828–8 (paperback)
  [1. Cats—Fiction. 2. Tigers—Fiction. 3.
Jungle animals—Fiction. 4.
Wizards—Fiction.] I. Ellis. Andy. II. Title.
PZ7. E2437Mi 1992   91–33201
[E]—dc20   CIP
                                                    AC

PRINTED IN ITALY

2345 0987654321

To Mandy and Owen,
J.E.

First edition for the United States and
Canada published 1992
by Barron's Educational Series, Inc.

Originally published by J.M. Dent and
Sons, Ltd, London, 1991.

Text copyright © Jim Edmiston, 1992

Illustrations copyright © Andy Ellis, 1992

All inquiries should be addressed to:
Barron's Educational Series, Inc.
250 Wireless Boulevard
Hauppauge, New York 11788

Jim Edmiston and Andy Ellis

Mizzy and the Tigers

Mizzy was the daughter of a wizard. She had hair the color of sunshine and bright blue eyes, and because she was the daughter of a wizard, she wore a cloak with moons and stars on it just like his.

She loved cats. The house was jam-packed full of them. Small, round, fat ones, and long, tall, hairy ones: skinny, soft, shiny, smooth, sweet-tempered, and bad-tempered ones.

The cats were always getting in the way. For
instance, if the Wizard was casting an important
spell, like trying to change an empty cookie jar into
one full of chocolate cookies (the kind he liked best),
a cat would always distract him. That meant he
would get his magic words mixed up, and the cookie
jar would end up full of friendly frogs or smiling
snails.

Mizzy's favorite cat, and also the biggest and stripiest, was Zigzag.

She often told him, "You are the biggest, stripiest cat in the whole world."

When he heard this, Zigzag would purr and purr.

But one day when Mizzy was stroking him and Zigzag was purring, the Wizard overheard her.

"I'm afraid he's not the biggest," he said, "or the stripiest. There are others—they live in the jungle. They are bigger and stripier and they are called tigers."

"That can't be true," said Mizzy, looking surprised.

"Oh, yes, it is," said the Wizard.

"Then I must go and see them," she said, for Mizzy was a cat lover and she had a mind of her own.

"But they're very big!" cried the Wizard.

"Good!" said Mizzy.

"And they can be very fierce!" howled the Wizard.

"I'm not scared," said his daughter.

"And . . ." said the Wizard slowly, making a knife and fork appear out of thin air, "they might eat you!"

"Don't be silly," said Mizzy. "Cats eat cat food. Everybody knows that!"

While the Wizard stood there, at a loss for words, Mizzy put on her jungle boots and hat. She put her knapsack on her back and off she went. Zigzag decided to stay home.

On the way, she saw an antelope grazing. He looked up quickly and his eyes seemed to speak to her.

"Beware of the lightning storms that pounce—they are the stripes of the tiger."

"Thank you," Mizzy said and walked on into the jungle.

Crossing a river, she met an elephant washing the dust off her wrinkled skin.

The elephant trumpeted, "Beware of shadows that run—they are the stripes of the tiger."

"Thank you," Mizzy said and walked on into the jungle.

Then, among some tall trees and dangling vines, Mizzy came face to face with a snake. It was one of those dangerous, squeezy ones, but, luckily, it had just finished lunch.

The snake hissed, "Beware of the long grasses that walk—they are the stripes of the tiger."

"Thank you," Mizzy said and walked on into the jungle.

Soon, eyes started to peer out at her from the long grass, and shadows moved between the trees. Then an enormous, tree-trembling roar cut through the air. It landed in front of Mizzy. It was a tiger! And it was big!

Another sprang out of the jungle, lowering its eyebrows and scowling in order to look as fierce as possible. It landed right beside the first one.

They both looked at Mizzy.

Every bug, bird and beast ran, crawled, hid or flew away as fast as it could. But Mizzy stood perfectly still. Quite calmly she opened her knapsack, and took out some cat food and offered it to the tigers.

"You are bigger than Zigzag," she told them, "and stripier."

The tigers looked at one another. They raised their eyebrows. They smiled, licked their lips and ate up all of the cat food. Mizzy invited them back for dinner, and to meet all her cats.

When she arrived home with the tigers there was quite a commotion. All Mizzy could see of her cats were their tails disappearing around corners and under chairs, and furry ears ducking down out of the windows and doors. Zigzag hid in the cupboard.

The Wizard cast a magic spell rather too hurriedly and got his words completely mixed up. He wanted to be swinging from a rubber tree but found himself swimming in a cup of tea!

Mizzy did her best to calm everyone down. She took some more cat food out of the refrigerator. The tigers agreed not to growl with their big, powerful, toothy, open jaws, and tried not to look too fierce. Soon all the cats began to reappear, and they all made friends.

Perhaps it had something to do with the magic of
the Wizard's house, or perhaps it was the kindness of
the Wizard's daughter, but the tigers were as good
as gold, and nobody worried about being eaten.

Mizzy went to bed the happiest cat lover in the
world.

 Late that night, by the light of the stars, the tigers
tiptoed out of the house, through the garden and
ran, leaped, and bounded the miles and miles back
to their own jungle.

When Mizzy woke up in the morning to find them gone, she was very upset.

The Wizard explained, "Small, stripy cats live in the house. Large, stripy cats live in the jungle. They have their own home, and must find their own food. They have their own way of doing things." Mizzy understood and began to cheer up.

Then he smiled and said, "Have a chocolate cookie." His spell had worked properly for once.

Just then Zigzag jumped up onto her bed. Mizzy hugged him and told him that, as far as she was concerned, he was still her biggest and stripiest cat, and Zigzag purred and purred and purred.